George Washington Snow

The Martyrdom of Jacques De Molay

the last grand master of the antique order of Knights templars - A

historical poem

George Washington Snow

The Martyrdom of Jacques De Molay
the last grand master of the antique order of Knights templars - A historical poem

ISBN/EAN: 9783337291792

Printed in Europe, USA, Canada, Australia, Japan

Cover: Foto ©Andreas Hilbeck / pixelio.de

More available books at **www.hansebooks.com**

THE

Martyrdom of Jacques DeMolay,

THE

LAST GRAND MASTER

OF THE

Antique Order of

KNIGHTS TEMPLARS.

—••—

A Historical Poem,

GEO. W. SNOW. K. T.

TO ALL

MASONIC KNIGHTS TEMPLARS,

WHEREVER DISPERSED,

THIS POEM

IS FRATERNALLY DEDICATED, BY

THE AUTHOR.

BENJ. A. BURR, PRINTER, BANGOR.

INTRODUCTION.

In the following Poem, the author has attempted to present, in a condensed form, the history of the events which preceded and caused the downfall of the Ancient Order which, for two hundred years, stood "the firmest bulwark of Christianity in the East, and saved Europe from desolation, if not from Turkish conquest."

These events occurred between A. D. 1291, the date of the fall of Acre, (the metropolis of the Latin Christians in Palestine,) and A. D. 1313, when the pope declared the Order abolished, and all its immense possessions throughout the dominions of France and the Holy See, were confiscated by the king and pope. The principal actors in this cruel drama, which commenced with the arrest and imprisonment in one night, of every Templar in France, including the torture of large numbers in their dungeons, and their death at the stake, on refusal to save their lives by confession of the guilt of the Order, and culminated in the martyrdom of De Molay, were Philip IV. of France and Pope Clement V., whom the king had raised to the pontifical chair through the intrigues of the French cardinal Da Prato, who acted as the king's secret partizan in the college of cardinals, during the struggle to elect the successor to Benedict XI.

In the progress of the drama the author has endeavored to represent these men as they appear in cotemporary history, where the ambition, unbounded avarice and revengeful disposition of Philip, and the venality, weakness and subserviency of Clement, are fully shown.

In regard to the course of Clement, the circumstances of his elevation to the popedom through the agency of the king, will sufficiently account for his acquiescence and aid in the execution of Philip's designs. It is evident, however, that he would gladly have saved the Templars from their final fate, but for another demand of Philip involving the infallibility and sacredness of the popedom itself, requiring that Clement should desecrate the remains of the dead pope Boniface, against whom the wrath of Philip was so intense and unappeasable, that he insisted that the body should be torn from the tomb, burnt, and the ashes cast into the Seine. To prevent this fatal sacrilege, Clement reluctantly acceded to all the other demands of the king.

It is hoped and believed that the historical events as described in these pages will be found interesting, not only to the members of the Masonic Fraternity, but to the general reader of history; and with this hope this volume is submitted to the public.

THE CONCLAVE.

When death had laid Rome's Pontiff in the dust,[1]

And selfish Bishops sought the vacant chair

Through secret intrigues, with unholy lust

Of low ambition—Philip, surnamed The Fair—

The vengeful, avaricious king of France,

Saw with glad eyes the Prelates at their game—

Saw too, and seized with eager hands, the chance

To win the power to do a deed of shame—

A crime that doom'd to infamy his name.

The while the Conclave, in Perugia met,

Kept up their selfish strife with jealous hate,

For Rome's proud throne, two factions therein sought,

By intrigue, artifice and stubborn will—
Nay, e'en with bribes these Holy Fathers wrought—
To win the lofty seat—but vainly still,
For disrobed cardinals, and under ban,[2]
Who had no voice within the College, fan
The angry discords, and with lavish gold
The even balance of the contest hold.

Thus, long divided in their Council, stood
These Holy Prelates, but their shameful feud
Had grown from causes far beyond *their* ken—
Hatred, revenge and pride of selfish men,
Whose hands in secret, guided and controll'd—
Moved, or restrained, by either craft, or gold—
These, their blind instruments, who but fulfil,
As passive tools, their unseen leaders' will.

It boots not here to seek what motives swayed

These differing partizans, who but obeyed

The selfish dictates of unhallow'd zeal,

Whose fires were fed by hatreds born of hell—

By fears, ambitions, bigotries—aye, all

The passions vile, that, venom-bloated, crawl

In the dark depths of man's perverted soul,

Whence all earth's myriad waves of wrong out-roll.

Th' unholy strife of these *most holy* men

Without abatement held its shameful reign ;

Days grew to weeks, but still appeared no hope

Of calmer counsels or a choice of pope,

Till days and weeks to many months increase,

Yet still these servants of the Prince of Peace

Kept up their wrangles, planned their idle schemes[3]

With a wild zeal, that to *our* vision seems

2

Inspired by him whose kingdom lies beneath,
Instead of the meek Man of Nazareth.

Within the conclave, well King Philip knew,[4]
Were priests of France—among its leaders too,.
Who, at his word would do, or utter aught
To aid the winning of the ends he sought.
These by Da Prato were most ably led—
A cunning priest, to Philip's interests wed.
A chief as shrewd the Roman faction claimed—
Francesco Gaetani, justly famed
For skill in intrigue, secret plot and scheme
With which the brains of reckless leaders teem,
And through these men, whom scruples troubled not,
The Monarch's power to name the pope is sought.

At length, of their long, fruitless contest tired,
Perugia's burghers, with impatience fired,

Around the Sacred College fiercely crowd,

With threat'ning words and clamorous voices loud,

Demanding that no longer be delayed

The choice of one, who, as the Church's Head,

Should mount her throne—that she no longer bear

The ills attendant on the vacant chair.[5]

Nor all unheeded by these cardinals,

The clamor of Perugia's people falls—

They saw and felt 'twere wise that voice to heed,

And not provoke its threat'ning into deed.

The Interview.

Night's deep'ning shades are o'er Perugia cast,

Another day of fruitless strife has pass'd

Within the Conclave. To their gloomy cells

Have gone the worn and weary cardinals.

In his dim chamber Gaetani walked,

Thinking aloud—for to himself he talked—

Of plans defeated—of his schemes o'erthrown,

In the long contest for the Papal Throne.

While thus the prelate, mutt'ring, trod the floor,

He heard approaching foot-steps near his door,

And soon a knock announced a visitor.

" Who seeks admission?" Gaetani cried—

" A Brother Cardinal," a voice replied.

Then Gaetani flung the portal wide,

And bade him "enter in the peace of God,"

And o'er the threshold, lo ! Da Prato strode.

Welcome and greetings o'er—" I come," he said,

" For thy wise counsel, hoping, with thy aid,

To find some means this fruitless strife to end,

Which doth, at length, beyond these walls extend ;

Rousing the people, who, with threat'ning voice

Demand without delay the Conclave's choice.

And well we know how cruel is the wrong—

E'en to all Christendom, that we so long

Have, by our fends, deprived it of its " Head."

" There are two parties," Gaetani said,

"In this long contest, and to all 'tis known

That one of these thy leadership doth own :

That I am counted with the other, I

Cannot, in truth, nor will I here deny ;

But not with us it rests—we look to you

For plan to break this stubborn dead-lock through."

" Brother Francesco, I have come to thee

Hoping thy wisdom might invent a key

To reconciliation's long-shut door,

And to our councils harmony restore :

That our Most Holy Church no longer be

A mark for scandal—prey to anarchy,

But by our action, on Her sacred Throne

Shall sit a Pontiff worthy of Her crown.

But, as thou dost *thy* plan to give, decline,

If thou wilt listen I will offer mine.

This my proposal then—a simple scheme,

And fair as simple, as thou can'st but deem.

We are divided, as thou'st truly said.

By differing views, by adverse interests led.

'Twere idle here to say this should not be,

That in our choice, there should, for you and me,

Be but one aim—the welfare to secure—

The honor and the glory to ensure

Of Mother Church and of the Holy See.

For we must take this matter as it stands,

And do what Duty's faithful voice demands.

Give, then, one party here the right to name

Three ultramontane cardinals[6] who claim

No seat within the Sacred College here—

Which will exclude one cause of jealous fear—

This done—the other from these chosen three

Shall make selection and on one agree,

Whom without question both shall then declare

The Conclave's choice to fill " St. Peter's Chair."

"Good Brother Cardinal, were't left to me

To act as umpire here,' I do not see

Aught in thy plan should cause me to refuse

My full assent thereto—I would not lose

A moment, but would have the compact sealed—

Our contest ended— our divisions healed.

But not with me, tho' fair it be, and wise,

But with my friends its full acceptance lies.

Them I'll consult, and I my promise give

For their approval earnestly to strive."

" Thanks, Gaetani, and with zeal no less,

My prayers to heaven shall rise for thy success."

With " *pax vobis cum* " doth Da Prato quit

Francesco's chamber, who, with words most fit,

Returned his courtesy, his "good night" said,

Murmur'd his prayers, and then upon his bed

3

Laid himself down, but busy thoughts long keep
From the tired Prelate's eyes, the balm of sleep.

Again 'tis morn, Perugia's golden spires
Reflect the glances of the solar fires—
Again her artizans—her sons of toil,
Speed to their labor—slowly now uncoil
The springs of Life, which Night and Rest have
To healthful tension with sleep's silent key ;
And Memnon-like on all the hills around
Floats the sweet music of Morn's minstrelsy—
Her joyous harmony all nature pours
Through myriad voices of her seas and shores.

The Sacred College does not meet to-day—
Wearied by months of intrigue and delay,
Both factions in the Conclave have agreed
To wait till known if Prato's plan succeed ;

For Gaetani hath the knowledge spread

Among the party of which he is head

And sought their counsel—learned their answer to

Da Prato's plan—he goes now to renew

The last night's conference.   Within his room

Da Prato waits, impatiently, the doom

Of his proposal ; but he waits not long—

Francesco's steps are hastening along

The corridor, and soon his welcome knock

Sends to his ear the echo of its shock.

The door swings back—he enters, and again

Sit face to face these holy, scheming men !

" What answer bring'st thou, Gaetani—say—

Do thy good friends accept, or not, the way

Out of our long resultless strife, which I

Did yesternight propose ?"   " This their reply,

They freely, fully to your plan agree,

With this condition :—That *they* name the three."

" Then be it so," Da Prato quickly said,

" And when the choice thou and thy friends have made,

Bring thou, my friend, the fateful list to me,

And in due time we'll name the Pope to be."

Three days have pass'd, and Gaetani stands

Again beside Da Prato, in whose hands

He places now the scroll wherein is writ

The chosen names the Roman priests submit ;

From which the Gallic prelates must make choice

Of one, which shall, without dissentient voice—

When meets the Conclave on th' appointed day—

Without, or question, cavil, or delay,

Become its choice, and it shall then declare

Its owner Master of St Peter's Chair.

For forty days the Conclave is adjourned,
And the tired cardinals have homeward turned.

Thus Da Prato's wiles succeed;
But, to make the prize secure,
He, a messenger of speed—
One whose faith and foot are sure,
Must dispatch without delay,
That the message on its way
Lag not, till in Philip's hand
Rests the all-important scroll.
Speed thee, bearer! win the goal,
Then reward may'st thou demand.

The wily Frenchman—prelate tho' he be,
Is a shrewd schemer too, as well as priest;
He hath foreseen, forestall'd necessity—
His courier started ere the bright'ning East

Gave earnest of the dawn.   Not in those years
The mighty Giant of the Iron Way
Sped o'er the land three hundred leagues a day,
Nor viewless Ariels, thro' earth's hemispheres
Out-stripp'd the sun, borne on the lightning's wing;
Yet did Da Prato's message reach the king
In briefest time—of days, just half a score
And one, for such a journey, was a thing
To make loud boast of in those days of yore.

THE SUMMONS.

Thus the Monarch won the key
To the door of destiny,
That opens to the way, wherein,
If he travel, he shall win
Full fruition of his hope—
Power to name the coming pope.
Aye, and bind him to fulfil
His behests, or good or ill.

Not an hour doth Philip wait,
Swiftly from his palace gate
Lo ! the royal courier rides—
Fleet the courser he bestrides.

Why and whither with such speed

Hasten now that man and steed?

Philip knows the urgent need,

And he sends that message forth

To the cardinal, De Goth[7],

The Archbishop of Bordeaux.

Tingle will his ears, I trow,

When that summons of the king

From the courier's lips shall ring.

THE COMPACT.

In an old Monastery, gray with time,

Deep in the shadow of St. D' Angely's wood,

As from its turret rang the vesper chime,

Philip before the blazing fagots stood.   ·

That up the broad flue sparkled joyously,

And sent their light and warmth the chamber through,

Rubbing, at intervals, his hands with glee,

Spreading their palms before the genial ray

Of the fire's rosy light.   Anon, he threw

Himself upon the couch beside the fire,

And leaning on his hand, lay list'ning there

And watch'd the dancing shadows' curious play

On wall and ceiling in the fire light glare.
  4

Alone he sat, but in the corridor
Waited and watched his faithful servitor
For Bordeaux's Bishop summon'd by the King
To meet him here—and hearty welcoming
Will greet his coming—but before they part
A heavy burden shall oppress his heart ;
For he is one among the chosen *three*,
And with the Monarch rests his destiny.
Not long his coming doth the King await—
E'en now the monks have met him at the gate,
And to the waiting page his steps they guide,
Who quickly leads him to the Monarch's side.

And now, within that chamber lone,
Sit Priest and Monarch—there the throne
Of Rome, her honors and her power,
All hang upon that fleeting hour ;

Aye, to be sold ere midnight toll

From the old Monastery bell—

Sold! and the price—a human soul!

And when that solemn chime shall swell

Upon the air, 'twill be the knell

Of a lost manhood, cheaply sold

As Esau's birth-right was of old.

Thus did De Goth before the King appear,

Ready to give a more than willing ear

To Philip's words, tho' to him yet unknown

The secret intrigues for the Papal Throne—

That in the Conclave long with discords rife,

The factious cardinals, to end their strife,

Into the monarch's hands the power had thrown,

On whom he would to place the Triple Crown.

Thus, to Bordeaux's Archbishop, spake the King :—

"Would'st thou be ruler o'er Rome's Holy See?

For if into thy scale my power I fling,

Thou'lt mount her throne—her mighty Pontiff be."

Quick fell his eyes toward the Monarch's feet,

That he might hide his look of keen desire,

And meekly answered : " Sire, it is not meet

That one so little worthy should aspire

To wield the scepter o'er Rome's mighty realm."

The King replied :—" Bernard, while I admire

Thy modest words, I know that at the helm

Of our Most Holy Church, thy steady hands

Would prove thee a most safe and trusty guide.

Within thy easy reach that scepter stands ;

Say, wilt thou grasp it ?   Hasten to decide,

For if the gift I offer thou dost spurn,

I doubt not one less modest I shall find

Among our cardinals, to him I'll turn

And raise him to the seat thou hast declined."

" O, Sire ! I pray thee deem me not the fool

To turn from such a glorious prize away ;

O'er Rome's vast interests worthily to rule—

Her Faith defend—her awful scepter sway,

A wiser man than I might doubt his skill.

Yet, if thy hand shall lift me to her throne,

To honor it and thee, doubt not my will—

Heaven will grant wisdom when it gives a crown."

" Reign even as thou wilt when thou art Pope—

I seek not now *my* honor, make it thine,

My worthy friend—my eyes have wider scope

And look beyond such petty motives—mine

Is not the hope of plaudits long and loud

From the rude rabble—the ignoble crowd—

No, my good Prelate—but if thou would'st wear

The Pontiff's honors, thou must boldly dare

To use thy power in aid of what I ask,

To its full stretch.   I warn thee, 'tis a task

Demanding energy, unyielding will.

Wilt give thy pledge, and given, wilt fulfil?"

The wary Bishop started as he heard

The King's proposal, and his heart was stirred

To fearful throbbings, while his eager eye

And trembling form betrayed the conflict high

Within, of hopes and fears, that sent amain

The heart's full current to the troubled brain.

But rallying soon, replied : " Disclose to me

The task to which my word and power must be

Pledg'd to perform, if to the Holy See

I shall attain by thy most gracious aid—

How and by what the debt must be repaid ;

And if, O Sire ! my soul it peril not,

Nor pass the limit of my utmost reach.

I give my promise, even tho' 'tis fraught

With many dangers—'spite of all and each,

Will I perform it, let what will impede—

As is my word e'en so shall be my deed."

" 'Tis bravely said, thy pledge is full and clear,

But words are breath, oft meant but for the ear—

From lips alone they issue, and the heart

In their light promises doth take no part,

And when we claim fulfilment, have no power,

For conscience speaks, or mem'ry may ignore

The hasty pledge, and therefore I demand

An oath, my good Lord Bishop, with thy hand

Upon the Holy Sacrament of God,

Which binds thy Order as a seal of blood!

In yonder pyx the sacred symbols are,

The eucharistic emblems, which "The Word"
Declares the blood and body of our Lord.
Now by their deep and awful mystery, swear
That thou wilt aid, with all the papal power,
The acts I purpose, in that coming hour,
When thou beneath St. Peter's sacred dome
Hast been crowned Pontiff of our Holy Rome."

But paused Bernard awhile, with down-cast eyes,
Then looking up, he said : "Thou dost not name
The task by which my hand may reach the prize."
"There's more than *one*, good Bishop, that will cl
Thy faithful service, but have thou no fear,
For all are worthy." "Then, Sire, I will swear."
Then kneeling, took the vow—his manhood sold !
Now did the King, in part, his schemes unfold,
But not the last and greatest, which he dared

Not even yet, to tell th' ambitious fool,

Whose venal soul his craft had thus ensnared

And made his willing—his subservient tool.

This did the monarch from De Goth withhold—

He must be pope and crowned e're that be told ;

Aye, till the king—his purpose ripe—shall speak

The fearful words shall blanch the Pontiff's cheek.

THE ELECTION.

De Goth has sworn upon the Sacred Host—
Crowned his ambition at a fearful cost—
Bartered his soul, and all his manhood lost.
Henceforth shall he the slave of Philip live,[8]
Whose sateless cravings, ever crying, "give!"
E'en like the horse-leech—shall fill all his life
With bitter trials and with inward strife.

And now, to make the king's decision known,
Without delay his courier hath borne
With swiftest speed, to where the cardinals
In Conclave sit within Perugia's walls,
And in obedience to the king's commands

Hath placed the message in Da Prato's hands,
Who quickly summons all his partizans
To private conference—to them makes known
The monarch's choice of Bernard for the throne.

And when the Conclave on the morrow meet—
As bound by "compact."—they the choice complete
By formal action.   Thus De Goth⁹ is made
Pope by the game the cunning Philip played.
How sped that game has been already told,
And how the king, much more by craft than gold,
The mighty power from jealous prelates won,
Thus for *their* choice, to substitute his own.

Now the Conclave's work is done—
Bernard's costly prize is won,
And the Gallic monarch smiles

At the triumph of his wiles—

Sees with joy, his evil sowing,

Fast to ripen'd fruitage growing—

Laughs to think that he who wears

Rome's proud crown—her scepter bears—

Must, subservient to his will,

Henceforth, as the *Pope*, fulfil

All, to which his fearful oath

Bound th' aspiring *priest*—De Goth.

But the name the prelate bore,

He, as Pontiff, bears no more—

" Clement "[10] shall, for praise or blame,

Bear thro' history his fame—

Justice render fitting meed,

Evil fame for evil deed.[11]

Two years have sped down Time's swift, silent river

Since to the king De Goth his manhood gave,

And, in his folly, bound himself forever,

To do hard, bitter tasks, as Philip's slave.

But tho' severe and irksome, each and all,

He hath performed them, as a faithful thrall.

Yet, there remains one dread condition still

Of that most fatal "Compact" to fulfil.

With calm, stern patience has the vengeful king

Waited for fitting time, unfaltering

In his dread purpose—waited for the hour,

In which to claim the Pontiff's mighty power

For the fulfilment of the awful vow

He made for the poor bauble on his brow.

Now the hand of Destiny

'Mid her realm of Mystery

Strikes the soundless knell of doom

Which, tho' not to mortal ear

May its dread vibrations come—

Swelling loudly on the air—

Telling its sad tale of fear—

Yet its voiceless prophecy

All fulfill'd the world shall see

What the doom, that silent knell

Now is telling to the hours

As their sands are running low?

Who the victims? What the wo?

If ye would know, then further list my tale

While I essay the myst'ry to unvail.

THE TEMPLARS.

Two hundred years, with all their countless train

Of deeds of good, or ill—of scenes of pain,

Or joy—a panorama dark with clouds

Charged with dread levin-bolts, whose gloom enshrouds

The fated Nations—or, else, bright with gleams

From a cerulean sky, whose golden beams

Of a fair heaven beyond do prophesy—

Have swept like shadows o'er the land and sea

Since 'mid the hills of Sacred Palestine,

The noble, brave, chivalric, pious Nine[12]

Laid the foundation of that Brotherhood,

Which led the Christian hosts through fields of blood,

In countless conflicts with the Infidel,

6

With most heroic and untiring zeal.

That Warrior-Order, of a world-wide fame—

"KNIGHTS OF THE TEMPLE OF JERUSALEM,"

Who gave their swords, their lives, without reward,

The Pilgrims on their dangerous paths to guard

Through the wild passes of the hills, which lay

Between the "Holy City" and the shore

Of Jordan's sacred stream, as, on their way

To bathe within its waters, or adore

At the "Thrice Holy Sepulchre"—The Blessed Shrine"—

They trod the mountain paths of Palestine.

Two hundred years ! O what a wondrous story !

Has the Historic Muse, with truthful pen

Inscribed upon her pages, of the glory

Of those brave "Warrior-Monks"—those stalwart men,

Whose march was ever in the battle's front—

The first to meet the foe—to bear the brunt

Of war's fierce onset on a thousand fields,

Where christian swords clashed upon Moslem shields.

Such were the Templars in those struggles long,

Along Judea's coast, her hills among,

The sacred "Banner of the Cross" to rear

O'er Salem's walls, the Crescent thence to tear,

With holy zeal, from pinnacle and fane,

And give her shrines to Christendom again.

And this the well-earned, honor'd name they bore :—

"Soldiers of Christ and Champions of the Poor."

Poets in all the ages, since their day,

Have sung in honor of their glorious name,

And Genius crown'd it with immortal bay,

And Hist'ry's pages well attest their fame.

How have two centuries changed their humble state

Since, at their altar first, they knelt and took

Those solemn vows, their lives to consecrate

To pious deeds—to meet the battle-shock,

As fearless champions of the Christian Faith.

Then, few and poor, but now, a countless host,

With wealth and power, and crown'd with Honor's
        wreath

By all the nations.   Kings are proud to boast

Of the grand title—"'Templar," and to bear

The noble name[13]—to lavish lands and gold

Upon the Order, and most gladly share

War's toils and perils 'neath "Beauscant's fold."[14]

He who hath gather'd Fortune's golden store

In rich abundance, will most surely find

A demon lurks amid the glittering ore ;

And the proud brow which wreaths of honor bind,

Will learn full soon, a deadly viper lies

Hidden among the garland's oaken leaves.

The demon Envy glares with hate-full eyes,

On all that fortunate Success achieves.

Thus fared it with the Templars.   They had grown

From the weak few to a vast host of power—

From poverty to wealth ; but 'twas not won

From conquer'd foes, but was the liberal dower

Of princely gifts, bestowed by princely hands[15]

As merit's meed, well earned and freely given

By Kings and Nobles, Lords of many lands,

Who deem'd themselves thus almoners of Heaven.

Yet not their wealth, nor yet their fame and power,

Had charged the threat'ning clouds that o'er them lower,

With deadly lightnings, waiting but the word

From the vindictive and revengeful King

To smite them to the death, ere shall be heard

The warning thunder of its heralding—

E'en as the white squall from unclouded sky,

Strikes the doom'd ship, while neither sky nor wave,

Gives sign of danger to the ear or eye,

And whelms the hapless crew in ocean's grave!

"Why, then," you ask, "the King's relentless hate?

Why 'gainst the Templars doth his anger glow?

Why arrogate the ministry of Fate,

And nerve his arm to strike such fatal blow?

What else than these have thus provoked his wrath

Against this Order of such high renown?

In what pursuit stood they across his path?

What crime committed 'gainst himself or throne,

For which their ruin only can atone?"

As cause for envy, these had each their part

But not alone, with hatred filled his heart ;

It was an act—(a crime by Philip deemed,)

Charged to the Templars, which had roused his ire ;

But which to *them* but simple fealty seemed

To "Mother Church," to whom a duty higher

Than loyalty to kings, they felt was due.

It was no treason 'gainst the Monarch's throne,

That they were charged withal, for they were true,

Both to the kingly and the Papal Crown ;

But that to Boniface, their moral aid

They gave, in his fierce contest with the King,

Which 'rose between them, when the pope essayed

To sever from all secular control,

All properties in which the Church had fee,

And all her goods and lands, and, of the whole

To be, himself, the one and sole trustee.

And not the Church alone—the Clergy too,

And all monastic bodies shared the same

Exemption from all burden, tax, or due

The King might levy. Such a right to claim,

Might well have set the Sovereign's heart aflame ;

For France, thus shorn of power to tax, would be

Driven, ere long, to helpless bankruptcy.

This gave the wound that rankled in his breast,

And roused his vengeance to its wild unrest.[16]

How lacking wisdom is Ambition's slave !

Tho' Fame's loud voice may rank him with the brave.

Aye—and how madly blind he rushes on

O'er bleeding hearts until the prize be won.

For, when his hand is stretch'd that prize to clasp,

It proves a phantom to his eager grasp.

But he, within whose heart of deadly ire,

Revenge has kindled his Gehenna fire,

By far out-runs ambition's swiftest fool

In folly's race, and wins a fatal goal.

When his intent—no longer *wish*, but *deed*—

Is passed recall, he sees the fiend that led

Him to that goal—beholds the precipice,

Beneath whose crags Remorse's black abyss

Awaits his fall, while pauseless on his path

Stalks a dread Nemesis, whose quenchless wrath

Sleeps not, but ever, like a fiend of hate,

Silent and swift pursues him to his fate !

Deluded fool ! a demon's dupe thou art !

Who gives thee now a scorpion in the heart,

Whose venom poisons all life's fountain there,

And whose sharp fangs its quiv'ring fibers tear !

7

But the revengeful monarch gave no thought

To what the path he blindly trod, might lead,

But heedless, hurried to the ends he sought.

Revenge, Ambition, and insatiate Greed,

The wolfish trio regnant in his soul,[17]

Urged him with all their fierce, satanic power,

With reckless haste, on to the fatal goal,

Impatient for the long-desired hour,

When Greed with eager hands the spoil may seize—

Revenge gloat madly o'er his victims' pain,

And proud Ambition crown himself with bays,

Where coils the viper that shall pierce his brain.

THE BETRAYAL.

To Clement at Bordeaux doth a courier bear

Most urgent letters from King Philip's hand ;

Of courteous tenor, and with pretence fair

Of ardent wishes, that the Holy Land

Be wrested from the haughty Infidel,

And that the sacred banner float again

O'er Shrine and Temple, wall and citadel,

In all the cities of Judea's plain.

"And to this end "—thus did the monarch write—

"Most Holy Father, we must seek the aid

Of the brave Templars.   Wilt thou then invite

Their most renowned Grand Master, and persuade

That valiant Knight,[18] with all convenient speed

To meet us here in Paris, that we may,

In this most weighty matter, as we need—

Have the wise counsel of a Chief, grown gray

In faithful service in our holy wars.

And such, be sure, thou fail not to declare,

In our esteem, the character he bears—

That from our councils, him we cannot spare."

Thus was the fatal snare by Philip plann'd,

Through the weak pontiff, set for De Molay;

For Clement saw not yet the iron hand

So gloved in courtesy—that to betray

The old Grand Master to a fearful fate,

Was the deep purpose of the crafty king,

Who thus, in specious flatt'ry veiled his hate

To lure the victim to the death-trap's spring.

For even now the fatal train he lays[19]

Which shall, ere long, to utter ruin sweep

The Noble Order, while he thus betrays,

With guileful words, that hide his purpose deep,

The unsuspecting chieftain to his fate.

Aye—even now his hirelings, at his word,

Are sowing seeds that soon will germinate

In the quick soil, and like the prophet's gourd,

By rapid growth, will soon shut out the light

Of sun-like Truth, for calumny doth find

In human hearts a soil adapted quite

To slander's rankest growth.   And, thus maligned

By these base, venal creatures of the king,

The Templars soon will taste the Upas-fruit

That from the seed of lying rumors spring,

Rank with the poison of its deadly root.

That there may be no failure to maintain

By proof, these slanders, with consummate fraud

The monarch frees from dungeon-cell and chain

A felon vile, with promise of reward ;

Who, tempted thus, swears to black, damning crimes

Committed by the Templars in their rites ;

And on *such proof* the royal robber aims

To confiscate all properties and rights

Of the doomed Order throughout his domains.

But he from Clement hides his base design,

And for the Templars he respect still feigns,

While for their ruin he prepares the mine,

Not e'en his trusted, secret tools may know

His hidden purpose—his intended blow.

The Disclosure.

And now, once more the King and Pontiff meet,

And Philip claims full payment of the debt—

The heavy debt, th' ambitious priest, Bernard,

For Rome's Tiara recklessly incurred.

Within the king's most private chamber now,

From interruption safe and list'ning ears,

Philip reminds Pope Clement of his vow ;

Who, with a pang and thrill of horror, hears

The king's disclosure of his dread design—

Destruction of the Templars ! and he shook

With undissembled terror, and his brain

Reeled with the shock, as with a ghastly look

In mute astonishment and fear he gazed

Upon the features of the monarch stern,

Who calmly said :—Why art thou thus amazed,

Most Holy Father?   Hast thou yet to learn

That this proud Order merits well the doom

I long have purposed, and for which thine aid

Is now invoked?   The Holy Faith of Rome

Beneath their feet contemptuously they tread,

With most accursed and blasphemous rites,

Within their secret chambers they receive

Their ignorant, deluded neophytes.[20]

Thou art that Faith's defender, and must give

This damning heresy its death-blow ere

Its rank growth bid defiance to thy power.

Strike then ! and promptly, and with me thou'lt share

Heaven's high approval in that triumph-hour,

When this proud Order, by our faithful zeal,

Of their dark crimes the penalty shall feel."

" Sovereign of France, thy words have struck my soul

With wild amazement and with horror deep !

As if along the cloudless heavens should roll

Loud-crashing thunder-peals, and lightnings leap.

False to the faith ! This Order so renown'd

For valiant deeds thro' twenty long decades !

Which in the battle-front was ever found

In all the contests of our eight Crusades !

It cannot be ! Thine ear has been abused

By the false tongue of calumny, I fear.

On what authority are they accused ?

And by what proofs does their black guilt appear ? "

" Proofs ! Dost thou think I would this charge have

    made

8

Lacking the means to buttress it with proof?

I were an archer little skill'd indeed,

To launch my shaft at game so far aloof

That it may greet my bootless shot with scorn.

Nay—Clement, doubt not, there shall be no lack

Of confirmation when the veil is torn

From their dark deeds.   The truth-compelling rack,

From their own mouths shall, by confession, make

All further proof superfluous—and then,

For their complete destruction, will remain

Nought but thy Bull, commanding the arrest

Throughout our realms, of these blaspheming Knights,

Who, in their secret orgies, make a jest

Of all that's sacred in Rome's holy rites."

" O King ! this charge, 'gainst men whose holy zeal

Has made their name so honored thro' the world—

Whose blood, whose treasure, for the church's weal

Have been so lavishly—so freely given,

When and where'er her banners were unfurled,

Who 'gainst her foes so faithfully have striven—

Should, to the portal of our judgment, come,

As came Bendocdar to old Antioch's towers,

What time he summon'd to her bloody doom

Syria's strong capital—with resistless powers—

A mighty force of proof, which should not leave

A doubt to bar conviction, most entire.

From idle rumor will the world believe

This Christian Order worthy of the fire?"

"What mean'st thou, Clement? Is my word, then,
    nought?

Have I not said this charge shall be maintained

To the removal of thine every doubt?"

"Aye, Sire, thou hast so said, but hast not deigned
To show on what that fearful charge is built—
Its adamantine base—its rock-built tower,
From whose high battlements the catapult
Of truth invincible, its blows shall shower
Upon the walls of their strong citadel
Of good repute, of high and broad renown
For pious deeds, of which two centuries tell
The wondrous tale.[21]   Can these be battered down,
Think'st thou, by means less potent, Sire, than these?"

O'er Philip's face a deathly pallor spread,
As if his heart a mortal pang did seize,
And from his lips the ruddy color fled,
As o'er his teeth they closed with firm compress.
Thus, for a moment, silent sat the king,
As if he strove against some keen distress,

Then, swift as lightning, from life's central spring.

Rushed to his brow again the crimson flood,

While rage gleamed fiercely from his flashing eye.

But the shrewd monarch curbed his angry mood—

Waited for calmness ere he made reply;

For Philip knew the venal Clement well—

Knew that with him he played a winning game;

For he held secrets which, were he to tell,

Would whelm the Pontiff with a bitter shame.

And with this thought his passion ebb'd away,

And pass'd the cloud of anger from his brow,

But a brief moment did he yet delay,

Gath'ring his forces for a heavier blow

To *Strike aside* the shield, which, o'er their head

The Pontiff held—for Philip knew, in vain

Would e'en his strongest efforts be essayed

To *pierce* that panoply—and, as again

The monarch speaks, he cares not to renew

The charge of heresy, nor does he claim

The pontiff's aid as guardian of the true—

The Holy Faith of Rome—his surer aim

To a more salient point directs he now ;

Not to Rome's Hierarch, her mitred Pope—

Ruler o'er Christendom—the Church's hope,

High Heaven's Vicegerent, under awful vow

To guard the Fount of faith and keep it pure

From heresy's polluting streams most foul,

But to the *man*—De Goth—whose sordid soul

He knew, would seize, with greedy haste, the lure.

"Clement ! hast thou forgotten, then, the hour

When thou and I met in St. D'Angely's hall?

Where thou did'st pledge to me thy future power

To aid my purposes?   Must I recall

Thy solemn oath, given on bended knee,

To do my bidding, if within thy hand

I placed the scepter of the Holy See?

Well—let that pass—I will not now demand

That oath's fulfilment, neither will I, here

Further debate the question of the guilt

Of these proud Templars—that will soon appear.

We'll waive all that, good Clement, if thou wilt,

And come at once to what I would propose—

'Twere idle now to try our thoughts to hide.

We know each other all too well, to gloze

With words whose meaning must be spoke "aside."

This haughty order whose full coffers groan

With hoarded gold, jewels and costly gems—

The gather'd wealth of years, wherein is shown

The steady flow of many golden streams

From many fools, to this all-swallowing sea—

Their broad domains, their power and lordly state,

Increasing ever, Clement, we can see,

Have made them insolent. Let us not wait,

Till stronger grown, they dare resist our sway.

Strike now—suppress the Order—seize their lands,

Their hoarded wealth. Thus shall we sweep away

Their o'ergrown power, then from their weaken'd ha

The golden spoil—of which *our thrones are heirs*[22]—

Shall to our coffers fall, and cease to be

The cause of jealous envy—for in theirs

It is, by privilege, exempt and free

From tithe or tax, or burden of the state.[23]

At this the people murmur—well they may.

Then act with me, nor longer hesitate.

Thou hast already summon'd De Molay[24]

From Cyprus hither. He and three-score Knights

Who with him come, are now upon their way—

For so my trusty emissary writes,

Whose letters from Limisso came to-day."

" Sire, I forget not—never shall forget

Our conference in St. D'Angely's abbey held,

Nor aught I pledged to thee when there we met;

Nor can'st thou charge that I in aught have failed.

Yet do I deem thou should'st thus much concede

To my desire to know whereon is built

Thy awful charge, on which I must proceed,

Ere has been tried the question of their guilt."

"Thou sayest well—I grant it were but just

That thou should'st have full warrant for thine act :

9

And as thou 'st met my charges with distrust,

Know that by good authority they're backed—

No less than this :— A Templar, on his oath,

Has of their truth confession made to me.[25]

This must compel belief, however loath,

And make all doubt give place to certainty."

" Enough, O King ! I will no longer strive

To shield these heretics, for thou hast given

A blow my strongest faith cannot survive.

Thou know'st I have against conviction striven,

But 'tis in vain—*confession* ends all doubt.

Thou art my witness, and can vouch for me,

That I most truly, earnestly have sought

To shield them from this damning infamy.

As thou hast said—our Holy Church doth claim

My utmost efforts, pure her Faith to keep

From heresies—to guard her from the shame—
The degradation of a sin so deep
As these blaspheming knights are charged withal ;
Nor suffer it a day unscathed to pass.
On the doom'd Order soon my blow shall fall,
And heavily as sudden—by the Mass !"

" Well hast thou spoken, Clement.   Give the word
For the arrest of every knight in France ;
And this a simultaneous act must be
Throughout our realm, lest some escape perchance ;
And for like reason use all secrecy."

Thus this reckless, vengeful pair
For their victims lay the snare.
Soon, within their dungeons lone,
Joint and nerve and reeling brain

On the rack—with vain appeal—

Madd'ning agonies shall feel.

They shall supplicate in vain,

Torturers will not heed their moan.

Venal Pope and treach'rous king!

Ye shall feel remorse's sting;

From your sowing there shall grow

Bitter fruit and fearful woe!

The Rack and Dungeon.

Slowly their weary round five years have roll'd

Since Gallia's despot and his mitred slave—

One in revenge and hate, and both for gold—

To dungeons dark, and torture-chambers gave

Those noble Warriors, old and battle-scarred,

From their long warfare on Judea's plains.

Where 'gainst the Crescent for the cross they warred.

Did such a service merit racks and chains?

Yet, such the guerdon which the Pope bestow'd

Upon those brave supporters of "The Faith"

Thro' the long struggles on those fields of blood,

Where countless thousands gave themselves to death,

To win the " Holy City," and to keep
Her shrines untrodden by the Infidel.
They sowed their blood on battle-fields, to reap
This bitter harvest of their prison cell ![26]
Harvest of pain !—of tortures most intense !
By fire and cord—the thumb-screw and the wheel !
Such these brave Knights receive for recompence,
For all their suff'rings for the Church's weal.

It were a task most sad and profitless,
The story of those torture-years to tell.
Let Fancy paint the scenes of dire distress
Where fiend-like men enacted deeds of hell !
Yet justice doth demand we pass not by
In wrongful silence here, that other tale—
How their keen agonies these warriors bore—
Their wondrous fortitude, that did not quail,

Tho' tortured e'en till fainting life gave o'er,

And tempted, too, by guileful promise given

Of absolution, life and liberty ;

Yet how few falter'd, and how few were driven

To gain, by false confession, even those ![27]

How many, steadfast, even unto death,

In silence died—yet triumph'd o'er their foes—

For martyr'd Truth may claim a victor's wreath.

And thus for years the fiendish torturers strive

To wring confession by the rack and wheel,

With all that bigot malice can contrive,

To wrench the sinews—make the reason reel.

And yet they win not from these victims aught

To fix upon the Order guilt or stain.

E'en at the "*Auto's*" flames they yielded not,

Tho' life and absolution they might gain,

But firmly met the martyr's fearful death—
Declared their innocence with latest breath !

In their lone dungeons, bound with heavy chains,
The few surviving Templars, weak and worn,
Had languished all these years—their cruel pains—
So long, and with heroic patience borne,
Had wreck'd their bodies and their souls benumb'd,
And courage died for hope no more sustained.
Thus in despair, what wonder *some* succumb'd
To Philip's power and made confession? Feign'd
A guilt they knew not, that they might be free
From fetters, tortures, and a living tomb ;[28]
That e'en Molay, in dire extremity,
By false confessions, sought to 'scape his doom ;
For Nature, in her mighty anguish, pleads
Too loud and strong for human fortitude.

The crush'd form yields—the broken spirit bleeds,

And Philip gains the end so long pursued,

For nought but feeble breath is left them now,

With little strength to frame it into words ;

And so, unto their torturers they bow

In mute assent—'tis all that strength affords.

But even *this* the King and Pope declare

To be confession of the Templars' guilt !

Wrung thus from them by torture and despair !

Yet, have these crowned and mitred tyrants built

On such foundation their nefarious scheme

Of wrong and ruin to these hapless men—

Their hope, that from this proof the world will deem

Their action blameless, and their course sustain.

For such the fame these Christian Knights have gained

Thro' two full centuries, for noble deeds

10

For Church and State—for loyalty unstained,

That 'twere not safe, even for crownéd heads,[29]

Without confession, recklessly to doom

These men to ruin, and their wealth to seize ;

And King and Pontiff dare not thus presume,

And hence their haste to make these mockeries

Of rack-wrung assent to their charge, appear

As full confession, to the people's ear.

Therefore, to crown their action with success—

Secure a vindication most complete,

The Templar Chiefs in public must confess

Before th' assembled people, and repeat

Avowals of their Order's guilt, as wrung

From them in dungeons—that these tyrants proud,

For their vile act of cruel, causeless wrong,

May win the sanction of the thoughtless crowd.[30]

For the bewilder'd multitude, in doubt,
Gaze 'round in fear, and in faint whispers ask
If these brave Knights, who have so boldly fought
For " Holy Land," have hid beneath a mask
False hearts of vilest hypocrites and knaves ?—
They—honor'd by the world as true and good,
Been false to all their vows—to lust been slaves !
As champions of the Church have they not stood
Through two full centuries, and true to all
Her interests, honor, and her awful sway?

Well may they ask, and marvel at such fall,
And look with wonder and in sad dismay
Upon the Order's ruin. Philip feels
And knows that peril in his pathway lies—
Knows that the Templars' cruel fate appeals
With mighty force for sympathy, that tries

The faith and fealty of Christian souls.

To guard against which peril—to forestall

The public judgment, he subservient tools

Finds in the "Friar Preachers"—one and all,

Of whom, with willing voices, at his call

Harangue the people on the Order's guilt.

And the king's Ministers in tones as loud,

Assail the Templars—heavy blows are dealt

In long addresses to the list'ning crowd,

Denouncing, black'ning, magnifying each

Vile charge of crime the king has falsely brought

Against these Knights. Their venom'd arrows reach

And wound their reputation, dearly bought

By faithful service of two hundred years ;

For Philip feels the urgent need to make

The Templars' guilt beyond all doubt appear,

Nor scruples he for this all means to take,

That every kindly impulse of the heart,

That rises ever at such awful woe,

May be crushed out, and pity take no part

To check or lessen the impending blow.

TRUTH ! mighty, glorious attribute of God !

Whereon all faith of men and angels rest—

All hope, that gives us strength to bear the load

With which our earthly being is oppress'd—

Which lifts the soul above all human fear,

And gives us victory even over death—

To view the stake the bigot-tyrants rear,

The block and headsman, with unwavering faith—

Well did the Persian Monarch speak of thee

As " mighty above all things," and declare :—

" Thou art the wisdom, beauty, majesty

Of all the ages ! Blessed be thy name
O'er all things else, thine is the victory !"

The early spring-time over sunny France
Has robed the fields with verdure and with flowers ;
The morning sun fills all the blue expanse
With glorious sheen, as he leads on the hours,
And marks their passage with his golden pen
Upon the dial, as they swiftly speed.
But e'er his zenith-station he shall gain,
He will look down upon an act, whose meed
Shall be, on History's page— a glorious name
Worthy a tablet in thy temple, Fame !

THE KING'S FAILURE.

From lofty balcony the king doth gaze,

With inward joy, upon the living tide

Of eager thousands, thronging all the ways

That stretch far out into the country wide ;

For, in obedience to *his* call they come,

That they may hear the Templars' crimes confess'd,

E'en by their Master, and approve the doom

Decreed by King and Pontiff, and attest

To all the Christian world, that this, their deed

Of greed and malice, was to justice due ;

That earnest zeal for Rome's most holy creed

Gives inspiration to the act they do.

In this assurance, Philip smiles to see
The gath'ring crowds the streets of Paris throng,
And, like a river speeding to the sea,
Towards the little islet rush along,
Whereon doth rise the Grand Cathedral pile—
The lofty towers of ancient Notre Dame
Above the parted current of the Seine—
Divided thus by famed Lutetia's Isle—
Forming a double mirror of the stream,
Whence are reflected, in day's golden beam,
Two wrinkled pictures of the Sacred Fane.

And now, in circles deep around the square
Which fronts the Grand Cathedral, press the throng ;
The anxious, eager, curious looks they wear,
Attest their interest and feelings strong,
In the sad drama, soon to culminate

In Philip's triumph o'er those noble men,

For whose confessions gloomily they wait,

On which depends the Templars' coming fate—

Which shall make infamous the Tyrant's reign.

Conspicuous in the scene, above the heads

Of the vast multitude a scaffold stands,

Upon whose platform a proud Bishop treads,

With the King's provost—both with willing hands

Ready to do what Church or State commands.

On either side, the grim, embodied threat

Of the relentless King and servile Pope—

Two martyr-stakes, with fagots near, are set,

To give this warning :—"Bid adieu to hope !

For the red flames await you, should ye dare

Retract confession, or refuse, or fail

To re-avow your Order's guilt.   Beware !"

11

How strong in truth were he who will not quail,
When Power vindictive threatens such a fate !

Hark ! 'Tis a trumpet's blast, that heralds now
The coming of a troop of martial men,
Behind whose ranks, with feeble steps and slow,
March De Molay, Geoffrey of Aquitaine,
Guy, Grand Preceptor, and Hugh De Peralt,
Weary and worn, and wearing heavy chains—
Their Tyrants' recompense for many a scar,
Which tell of wounds received on Judah's plains,
In bloody contest with the church's foes.

Thus led and follow'd by their guards—with pains
Born of their dungeon-racks and many woes—
Towards the scaffold stairs they move along—
Each step a torture, and each breath a groan—
And reach, at length, their place above the throng,

On the high platform, which shall prove a throne

To two, at least, of those heart-broken men,

Whom Truth shall crown with her bright diadem

Of fadeless glory, whose immortal sheen

Shall far transcend their tyrants' richest gem.

Surrounded by the creatures of the King

And servants of the Pontiff, now they sit,

While from the mouth of Alba's Bishop ring,

In scornful tones, what venal priests have writ

As *free* confessions by the Templars made—

Albeit, extorted by the torturer's cord!—

Acknowledgement of acts that would degrade

Of Afric's lowest race the vilest horde!

And now, with voice imperious and loud,

The Papal Legate on the Templars calls,

Demanding that these acts be re-avowed,

As once confess'd within their prison walls.

How shall they answer?   Hardly have they breath

Or strength remaining, e'en for brief reply ;

And well they know th' alternative is death,

Should they refuse confession, or deny.[31]

Silent and listless, with eyes downward bent,

They sit, as if unheard that stern demand,

Until, with anger and impatience blent,

The wrathful Legate utters his command

With louder voice, and fiercely stamps the floor,

Which their attention to his words recall.

Two of these weary Templars lack the power

To do aught else than nod assent to all

The Legate's questionings, and thus reply

Geoffrey and Hugh Peralt[32]—but not Molay !

Nor did the noble Grand Preceptor, Guy,

For they had come with firm resolve to die,

For Truth to suffer, and their lives to lay

Upon her altar ; and, inspired by this,

De Molay's form received new strength to rise,

E'en with his load of chains, and thus address,

With voice unfalt'ring and unswerving eyes,

The mighty multitude, awaiting there,[33]

His answer to what haughty Alba claims—

Confession of that catalogue of crimes

Most infamous, which Pope and King declare

Alone shall save them from the " Auto's " flames.[34]

The Triumph of Truth.

———

" A captive long within your dungeons lone,

Bound with your chains, and tortured to the verge

Of life's endurance, by which ye have won,

From Nature's agonies, that which ye urge

Me and my Fraters, broken down with pain

And with the threat of death, embodied there

In yonder fagots piled with stake and chain,

To now acknowledge to the public ear

As truth most absolute ! O ! Thou whose eye

Searcheth the secret chambers of the soul,

Be Thou my witness from Thy throne on high,

While I declare each charge a slander foul—

Its substance falsehood and its root a lie !

And in this truth, O ! give me strength to die !

Yet, to my shame do I avow my guilt,

In that I yielded, e'en 'mid tortures keen,

To gain a respite from the pangs I felt—

A brief remission of the cruel strain

That wrench'd the sinews of my quiv'ring frame—

A half-unconscious, false acknowledgement

Of the vile crimes our enemies proclaim

Against our guiltless Order, to whose fame

Two hundred years have growing lustre lent."

Again stern Alba's angry voice is heard—

"Hold ! thou false Templar ! lying knave, no more !

Blister'd shall be thy tongue for each false word

Which thou hast uttered.   Thou hast dared abjure

Thy former true confessions, and accuse

Even the Holy Father and the king,

And us, their servants, and thou shalt not lose

Thy recompense, for ere the sun shall fling

His evening rays upon yon lofty Dome,

At yonder stake, amid the flaming fire,

Thou'lt meet the fate reserved for foes of Rome,

Who, like thyself, dare thus provoke her ire."

" I knew my fate when I was summon'd here

To stain my soul with falsehood, and I scorn

To save this life—this weary form I bear,

From Clement's doom—'tis of all terror shorn.

I see your stake, your chains and fagots there,

But to my inner consciousness appears

Truth's glorious form, whose radiance fair

Hides all their ghastliness. My spirit hears

Her voice that silences your threat of death

12

So loudly utter'd, ringing thro' the air,

And I again, e'en with this failing breath,

My Order's innocence do here declare—

No stain of guilt does their escutcheon bear."

And Guy, the Grand Preceptor, now essayed

To echo the bold words of De Molay,

But the indignant Legate now forbade

All further speech, and, to their cells, away

Both noble knights were hurried.   To the king

A speedy messenger doth quickly bring

Th' unwelcome tidings, and his anger rose

To a fierce heat of passion, and he throws

Aside all reason, all restraint, all thought

But that of vengeance, and he scruples not,

Without the Pontiff's sanction, to decree

The death by fire of Guy and De Molay!

But ere around their forms springs up the fire,

Speaks De Molay, as by the fatal pyre

He stands—turned on the multitude his look—

Who, awe-struck at the scene, in silence gazed,

And as he uttered, with his hands up-raised,

His dying words, like an electric shock,

A mighty shudder ran thro' all the crowd,

As from his lips this fearful summons flowed :—

" Oh Philip ! I forgive thee all my pain,

But well I know *my* pardon is in vain,

For thou art doomed, and ere a year has flown

I summon thee to meet me at the Throne

Of the All-righteous Judge of Earth and Heaven :

There learn if crimes like thine may be forgiven !

And thou, Oh Clement ! ere the circling sun

His round diurnal forty times has run,

Thou too art summon'd to that Judgment seat,

Us, the wrong'd victims of thy power, to meet.[35]

Guiltless we die, but thy unjust decree,

That dooms us here, at that High Court shall be

Reviewed by Him whose wisdom never errs:

There shall your wrongful verdict meet reverse."

Then, as they bound him to that fatal stake,

His voice once more is heard—but now he spake

Not unto *man*, but unto Him whose ear

Is ever open to man's humble prayer;

And in the spirit of the Crucified,

With trembling voice and tearful eyes, he cried:

"Receive our souls, Oh God! Forgive these men

Our cruel tortures and our death! Amen."

Thus died the noble martyr, De Molay—

True to his God, his Order, Truth and Right.

Which deem ye victor?　Think ye it was they—
The vengeful tyrant, with his power to smite.
And he, the puppet Pope—the monarch's slave?
Nay!　King and Pontiff suffer'd sore defeat
When perished thus those martyrs true and brave.
For 'twas a failure, surely, most complete,
When their false charges were thus overthrown
By stern denial with their latest breath.
Aye! they did win the victor's glorious crown,
When for the Truth they went to such a death.

EXPLANATORY NOTES.

1. Pope Benedict XI, A. D. 1304.

2. The Colonna family, who had been stripped of their power as Cardinals, by Boniface VIII.

3. On the death of Pope Benedict XI, 1304, King Philip succeeded, through the intrigues of the French Cardinal Dupre (or Da Prato), in raising the Archbishop of Bordeaux, a creature of his own, to the pontifical chair."—*Addison's K. T., p. 405.*

4. The interregnum of the Popedom continued two years.

5. A historical fact.

6. Northern Prelates—not Italians.

7. Bernard De Goth—or De Gott, as given by some writers.

8. "In all his acts, the new Pope manifested himself the obedient slave of the French monarch."—*Addison, p. 405.*

9. The character of this man has been painted by the Romish ecclesiastical historians themselves, in the darkest colors: a knave, a murderer, and a vile extortioner."—*Addison's K. T., p. 405.*

10. The new Pope was consecrated at Lyons by the name of Clement V., A. D. 1305.

11. The character of Clement is described by Roman historians to be that of a "knave, murderer, and vile extortioner."—*Addison's K. T., p. 405.*

12. Their names, as given by some authorities, are Hugh de Payens; Godfrey de St. Aldemar, (often written St. Omer;) Raoul Gundomar; Godfrey Bisol; Payens de Montidier; †Archembold de St. Amon; †Andre de Montbar, and Hugh, Count de Provence. *Wilcke, quoted by Milman, vol. vi, p. 334.* Addison gives these †two, Odo de St. Amand and Andre de Montbard.

13. "Many illustrious persons, on their death-beds, took the vows, that they might be buried in the habit of the order."

"Sovereign princes, quitting the government of their kingdoms, enroled themselves amongst the Holy Fraternity, and bequeathed even their dominions to the Master and brethren of the Temple."—*Addison*, p. 154.

14. The Beauseant—The Battle-Flag of the Templars—was formed of black and white cloth, and was first flown under the sky of Judea, where for nearly two hundred years its presence carried dismay into the ranks of the Infidels, who fled like sparrows from a hawk, on its approach. 'Tis strange, the power this flag had over the minds of both friend and foe. By the one it was looked upon as the talisman of victory, by the other, as the thunderbolt of destruction.—*Addison's K. T.*, p. 288.

15. Princes and nobles, sovereigns and their subjects, vied with each other in heaping gifts and benefits upon them, and scarce a will of importance was made without an article in it in their favor.—*Addison*, p. 154.

16. Pope Boniface VIII was possessed, even to infatuation, with the conviction of the unlimited, irresistible power of the Papacy.

He determined to bring to issue, once for all, the inevitable question, to sever the property of the Church from all secular obligation—to declare himself the one executive trustee of all lands, goods and properties held throughout christendom by the Clergy, the monastic bodies and the church, and that without his consent no aid, benevolence, grant, or subsidy could be raised on their estates by any temporal sovereign in the world. Such is the full and literal sense of the famous Bull of Boniface, at the beginning of the second year of his pontificate.

This famous Bull of Boniface was received by Philip with the greatest indignation. It struck at once at his *pride*, his *power*, his *cupidity*. Philip, of his sole will, had imposed the tax, and his wrath at the Pope's Bull was vehement, but his revenge was cool and deliberate. It was a retaliation which struck the Popedom deeply, and in the most vital and sensitive part. Philip issued an ordinance prohibiting in most rigid and precise terms, the exportation of gold, silver, gems, provisions, arms, horses, or munitions of war, or any article of current value, without his permission, sealed and delivered by the Crown.—*Milman's Latin Christianity, V. VI., pp. 259—266.*

17. The character of Philip is portrayed by Addison, as that of a needy and avaricious monarch, who had at different periods resorted to the most violent expedients to replenish his exchequer.—*p. 405.*

18. "We order you," says he, "to come hither without delay, *with as much secrecy as possible, and with a very little retinue,* since you will find on this side the sea a sufficient number of your Knights to attend upon you." De Molay forthwith accepted the summons, and unhesitatingly placed himself and his treasury in the power of the Pope and the King of France.—*Addison, p. 406.*

19. In the year 1307, the secret agents of the French king began to circulate various dark rumors and odious reports concerning the Templars."—*Addison's K. T., p. 406.*

20. King Philip, on the 14th of September, 1307, dispatched secret letters to all the Baillies of the different provinces in France, accusing the Templars of infidelity, of mocking the sacred image of the Saviour, of sacrificing to idols, and of abandoning themselves to impure practices and unnatural crimes.—*Addison, pp. 407 and 428.*

21. The Order partook of the sanctity which invested all religious bodies. They were, or had been the defenders of the Holy Sepulchre of Christ, and had fought, knelt and worshiped in the Holy Land.—*Milman, Lat. Ch., V. 6., p. 400.*

22. "The chief cause of the ruin of the Templars was their extraordinary wealth. As Naboth's vineyard was the chiefest ground of his blasphemy, and as in England, Sir John Cornwall, Lord Fanhope, said merrily, not he, but his stately house at Ampthill, in Bedfordshire, was guilty of high treason, so certainly, their wealth was the principal cause of their overthrow. We may believe that Philip IV would never have taken away their lives, if he might have taken their lands without putting them to death; but the mischief was, he could not get the honey unless he burnt the bees."—*Fuller, as quoted by Addison. page 419.*

23. "A. D. 1254—55, ten Bulls were published in favor of the Templars, addressed to the Bishops of the Church Universal, commanding them to respect and maintain the privileges conceded to them by the Holy See; to judge and punish all persons who should dare to exact tithe from the Fraternity."—*Addison, p. 373.*

24. At the death of Grand Master Gaudini. who died A. D. 1295, at Limisso, in the island of Cyprus. James De Molay,—(or Jacques De Molai, as often written) succeeded to the Grand Mastership of the Order. He was the twenty-second and last Grand Master of the antique series. This illustrious nobleman was of the family of Longvic and Raon, in Burgundy, and at the period of his election to the dignity of Grand Master, was at the head of the English province of the Order. Shortly after his election, he proceeded to Cyprus, carrying out with him a numerous body of English and French Knights Templars and a considerable amount of treasure.—*Addison, pp. 397—417.*

25. According to some writers, Squin de Florian, a citizen of Bezieres, who had been condemned to death, or perpetual imprisonment for his crimes, was brought before King Philip, and received a free pardon and was well rewarded, in return for an accusation on oath, charging the Templars with heresy, and with the commission of horrible crimes. According to others, Nosso de Florentine, an apostate Templar, who had been condemned by the Grand Preceptor and Chapter of France, to perpetual imprisonment for impiety and crime, made a voluntary confession, in his dungeon, of the sins and abominations charged against the Order. Thus, upon the strength of an information, sworn to by a condemned criminal, King Philip sent letters to all the provinces accusing the Templars.—*Addison's K. T., p. 406.*

26. They were handed over to the tender mercies of the brethren of St. Dominic, who were the most refined and expert torturers of the day. *Addison. p. 409.*
Many Templars perished in the hands of their tormentors.—*i. b.*

27. Fifty-four Templars were handed over to the secular arm, and were led out to execution by the King's officers, at day-break, into the

13

open country in the environs of Paris, and were fastened to stakes driven into the ground and surrounded by fagots and charcoal. In this situation they saw the torches lighted and the executioners approaching to accomplish their task, and were once more offered pardon and favor if they would confess the guilt of the Order, but they maintained its innocence, and were burnt to death before slow fires!—*Addison's K. T. p. 412.*

28. One hundred and forty were separately examined, * * * brought up from their dungeons without counsel, mutual communication, or legal advice, and subjected to every trial which subtlety or cruelty could invent, or which could work on the feebler or firmer mind. Shame, terror, pain, the hope of impunity, of reward—confession was bribed out of some by offers of indulgence—wrung from others by the *dread* of torture—by *actual* torture, with the various ways of which our hearts must be shocked, that we may judge more fairly of their effects.—*Milman, Lat. Ch. V. 6, p. 402.*

" As pardon and forgiveness had been freely offered to those Knights who would confess, it was not wonderful that false confessions had been made."—*Addison, p. 411.*

29. "It was prudent, if not necessary, to crush all popular sympathy; to leave no doubt of the King's justice, or suspicion of his motives in seizing such rich and tempting endowments."—*Milman, V. 6. p. 400.*

30. The whole clergy and the people were gathered together in the gardens of the Royal Palace. Sermons were delivered by the most popular preachers—the Friars; addresses were made to the multitude by the King's ministers, denouncing, blackening and aggravating the crimes of the Templars. No means were spared to allay any possible movement in their favor.—*Milman, V. 6, p. 400.*

31. A letter, sent to the imprisoned Knights at Sens, warned them against a retraction of their confessions (under torture) in the following words:

" Take notice, that the Pope has given command that they who have made confessions before his Legates, and do not persevere in these confessions, shall be committed to damnation and destruction by fire."—*Addison. p. 411.*

32. Hugh de Peralt, the Visitor General, and the Preceptor of the Temple of Aquitaine, signified their assent to whatever was demanded of them, but the Grand Master, raising his arms bound with chains towards heaven, and advancing to the edge of the scaffold, declared in a loud voice, that to say that which was untrue, was a crime, both in the sight of God and man. "I do," said he,—"confess my guilt, which consists in having, to my shame and dishonor, suffered myself, through the pain of torture and fear of death, to give utterance to falsehoods, imputing scandalous sins and iniquities to an illustrious Order, which hath nobly served the cause of Christianity. I disdain to seek a wretched and disgraceful existence by engrafting another lie upon the original falsehood." He was here interrupted by the Provost and his officers; and Guy, the Grand Preceptor, having commenced with strong asseverations of *his* innocence, they were both hurried back to prison.—*Addison, p. 416.*

33. See *Addison's Knights Templars, p. 418.*

34. "Auto da Fe"—Act of Faith—The burning of heretics.

35. A year and one month after the execution of the Grand Master and Grand Preceptor, Clement was attacked by disease, and was soon hurried to his grave. His dead body was conveyed to Carpentras, where the Court of Rome then resided. It was placed at night in a church, which caught fire, and the mortal remains of the Holy Pontiff were almost entirely consumed.

Before the close of the same year, Philip IV died of a lingering disease which had baffled all the art of his medical attendants, and the condemned criminal, on whose information the Templars were originally arrested, was hanged for fresh crimes. Clement, died April 20, Philip, Nov. 29, 1314.—*Addison, pp. 418—419.*

"History attests," says Raynouard, "that all those who were foremost in the persecution of the Templars, came to an untimely and miserable death."

The last days of Philip were embittered by misfortune. His nobles and clergy leagued against him to resist his exactions.

www.ingramcontent.com/pod-product-compliance
Lightning Source LLC
Chambersburg PA
CBHW032200010726
47493CB00008BA/2760